by Mariah Balaban

ISBN–13: 978-0-545-11415-8
ISBN–10: 0-545-11415-2

Cover and interior illustrations by Duendes del Sur

Designed by Michael Massen

12 11 10 9 8 7 6 5 4 3 2 1 9 10 11 12 13 14/0

Printed in the U.S.A.
First printing, May 2009

SCHOLASTIC INC.
New York Toronto London Auckland Sydney
Mexico City New Delhi Hong Kong Buenos Aires

Scooby and the gang were at the Coolsville Robot Expo.

"Gang, this is Professor Tinkerwell," Velma introduced her old teacher to the gang.

"I'm delighted to have you kids as my guests," he said. "Call me Doc."

Doc showed the gang around the robot expo. There were hundreds of different kinds of robots.

"Groovy! This robot can choose the right accessories for any outfit!" exclaimed Daphne.

"This dude can make a different pancake for every day of the year!" said Shaggy.

Doc took the gang to see his latest invention, the Battling Monsterbots.

"Rikes! *Ronsterrots*?" yelped Scooby-Doo.

"Don't worry, kids, my Monsterbots are perfectly harmless — unless you happen to be another robot!" Doc joked.

Suddenly, a man in a suit appeared. "Doc, if you know what's good for you, you'll sell me your Monsterbots! We can both make a bundle!" he shouted.

"Jeepers! Who's that?" asked Velma.

"This is Sy Smiley," Doc said. "He wants to buy my robots and sell high-priced tickets to the Monsterbot battles. But my robots are for everyone to enjoy, free of charge!"

"You'll sell to me . . . or else!" muttered Sy Smiley.

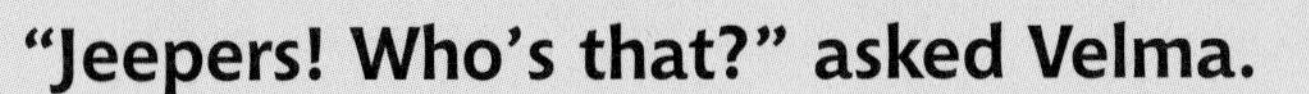

"People bring their robots from all over the world to battle Doc's Monsterbots," explained Velma. "The Monsterbots are practically unbeatable because they can change their shape!"

"Professor Tinkerwell stole that idea from me!" a man shouted. "I, Viktor Rustoly, am the true inventor of the Monsterbot! Tinkerwell will admit it or I'll make him pay!"
"Like, I think that guy's got a few screws loose!" said Shaggy.

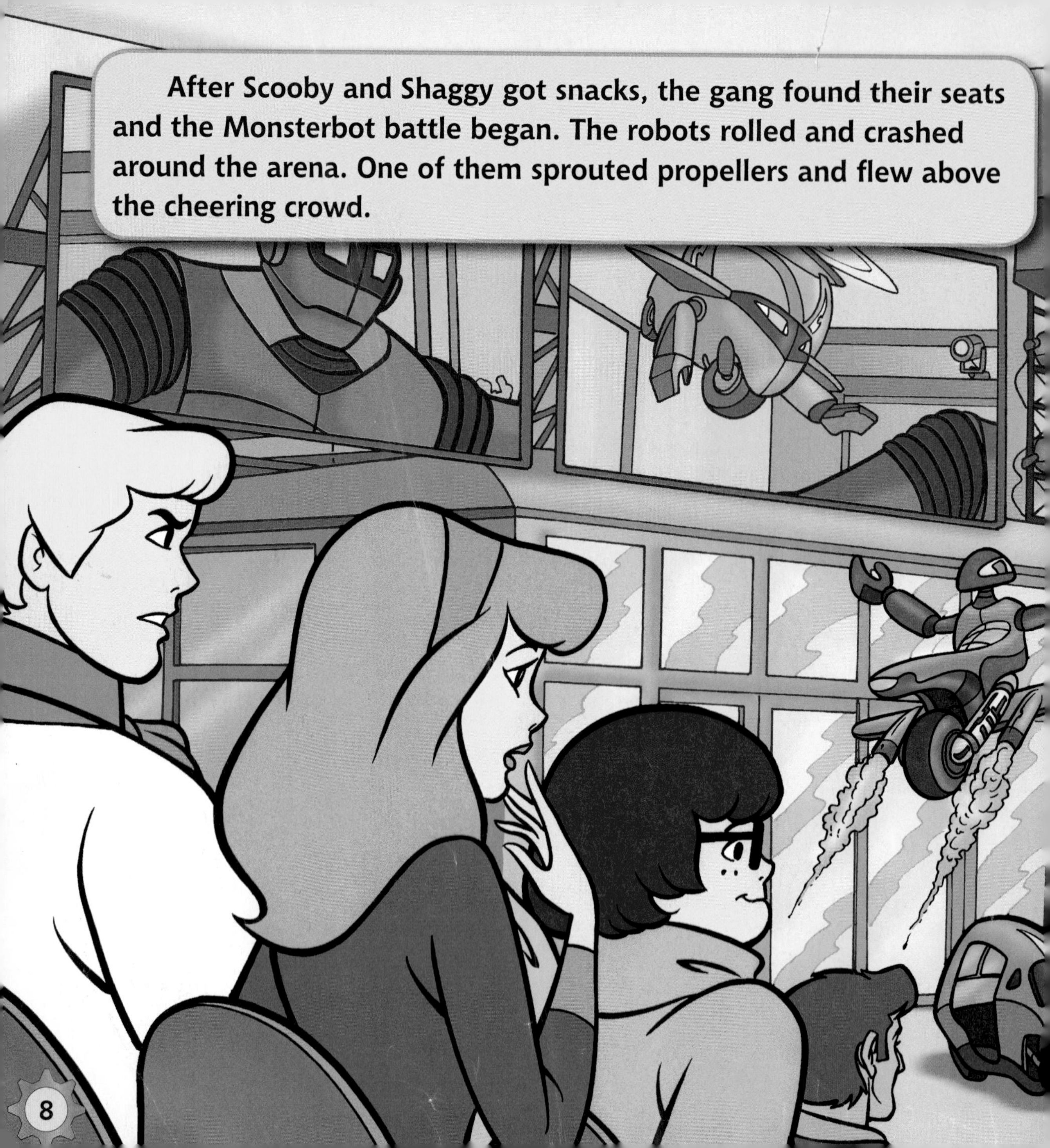
After Scooby and Shaggy got snacks, the gang found their seats and the Monsterbot battle began. The robots rolled and crashed around the arena. One of them sprouted propellers and flew above the cheering crowd.

For the grand finale, a huge robot stomped out.
"Like, I'd hate to meet him in a dark alley," Shaggy whispered.
"It looks like there's something the matter with that big Monsterbot. He's headed straight for the crowd!" exclaimed Fred.

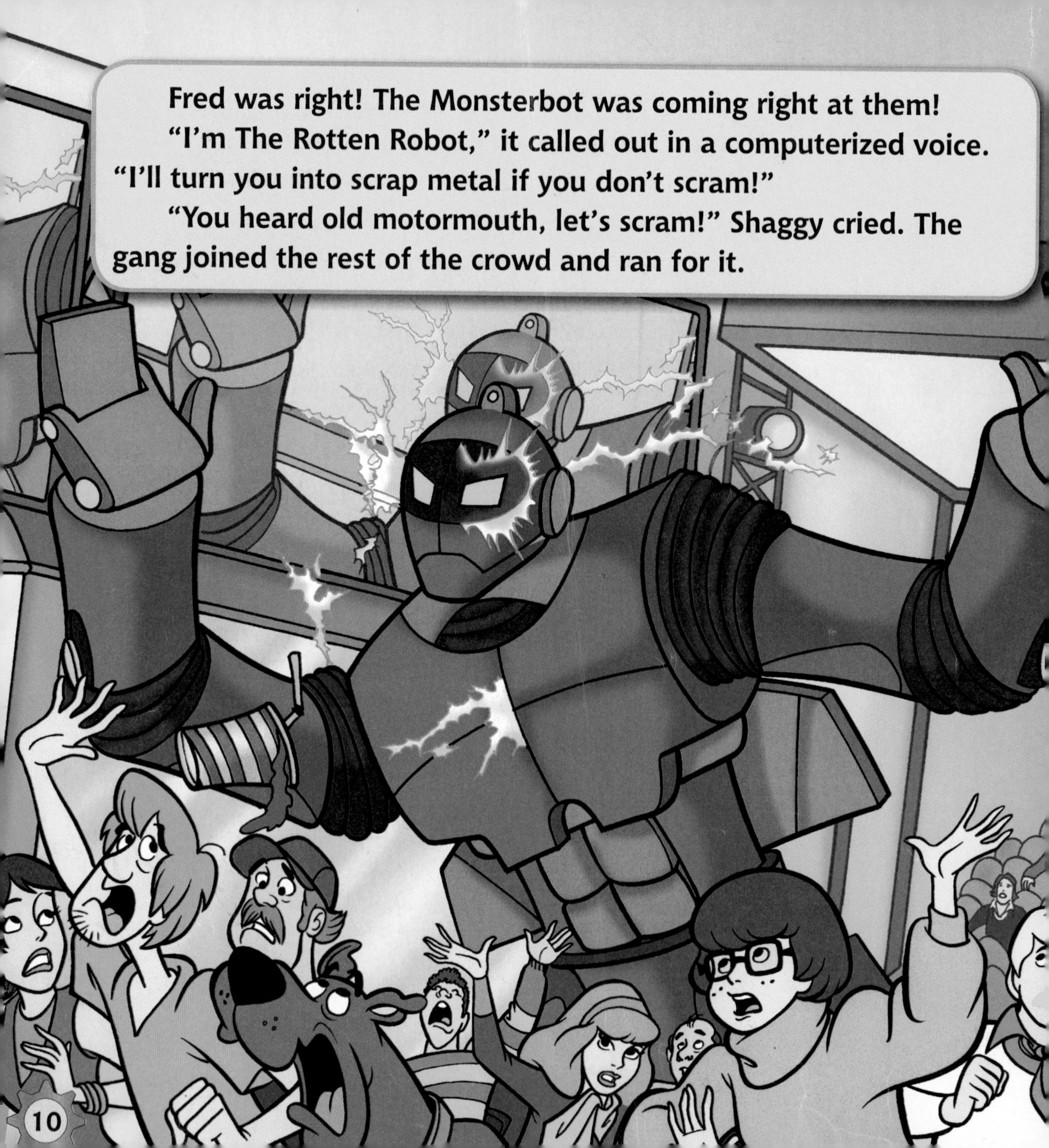

Fred was right! The Monsterbot was coming right at them!

"I'm The Rotten Robot," it called out in a computerized voice. "I'll turn you into scrap metal if you don't scram!"

"You heard old motormouth, let's scram!" Shaggy cried. The gang joined the rest of the crowd and ran for it.

The gang found Doc Tinkerwell backstage in his workshop. “If people think that my Monsterbots are dangerous, I’ll be ruined! You have to help me prove that I’ve been sabotaged!” Doc begged the gang.

“Don’t worry, Doc,” said Fred. “Mystery, Inc. is on the case!”

The gang decided to split up and look for clues. Daphne, Velma, and Fred went to check out the entrance to the arena.

"Hey, look at this!" exclaimed Velma, waving a piece of white cloth. "It's our first clue — Sy Smiley's handkerchief!"

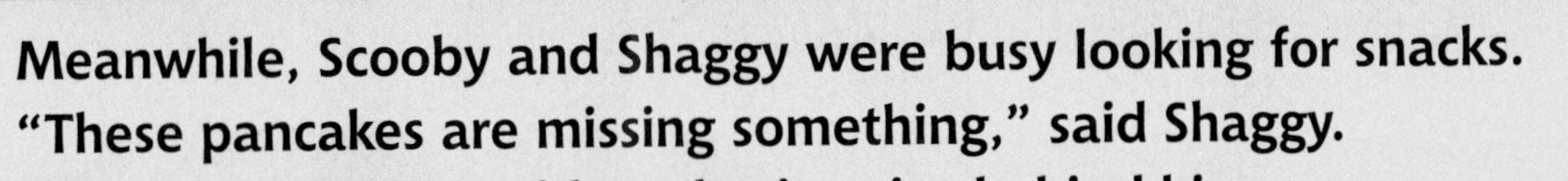

Meanwhile, Scooby and Shaggy were busy looking for snacks.
“These pancakes are missing something,” said Shaggy.
“Try some syrup?” said a robotic voice behind him.
“Good idea!” Shaggy replied. “But what’s with the funny voice?”
“Rorot!” barked Scooby. “Run ror rit!”

The Rotten Robot chased Shaggy and Scooby through the expo hall.

"Like, where's the off-switch on this rotten rust-bucket?" Shaggy asked.

Scooby and Shaggy finally lost the Monsterbot and found the rest of the gang.

"You're just in time, guys," said Daphne. "Look what we discovered!"

Fred, Daphne, and Velma showed Scooby and Shaggy robot parts and a toolbox. "We found a page from Viktor Rustoly's notebook in it!" Fred exclaimed.

"Did you guys find any clues?" Daphne asked Shaggy and Scooby.

"Like, does it count if the clue found us?" asked Shaggy.

The Rotten Robot had caught up with them again.

"When I catch you, I'll grind you in my gears," The Rotten Robot called after them.

"Is it just me, or does he sound a little cranky?" Shaggy joked.

The gang turned a corner and ran through a set of doors.
Shaggy and Scooby crashed into a shelf full of pots and pans.

"Gang, this stuff gives me an idea for a plan to trap that overgrown bag of bolts!" said Fred. "Scooby and Shaggy, you'll be robot bait."

"Ruh-roh!" barked Scooby.

Back in the Monsterbot arena, Doc Tinkerwell announced the next battle over the loudspeaker.

"Introducing the newest Monsterbot challengers: Team Scoobytron!"

The sound of crunching metal got louder and louder. . . . The Rotten Robot had come back, just as Fred had planned.

"I'll crush you like tin cans and use you for spare parts!" The Rotten Robot cried.
Fred gave the signal.

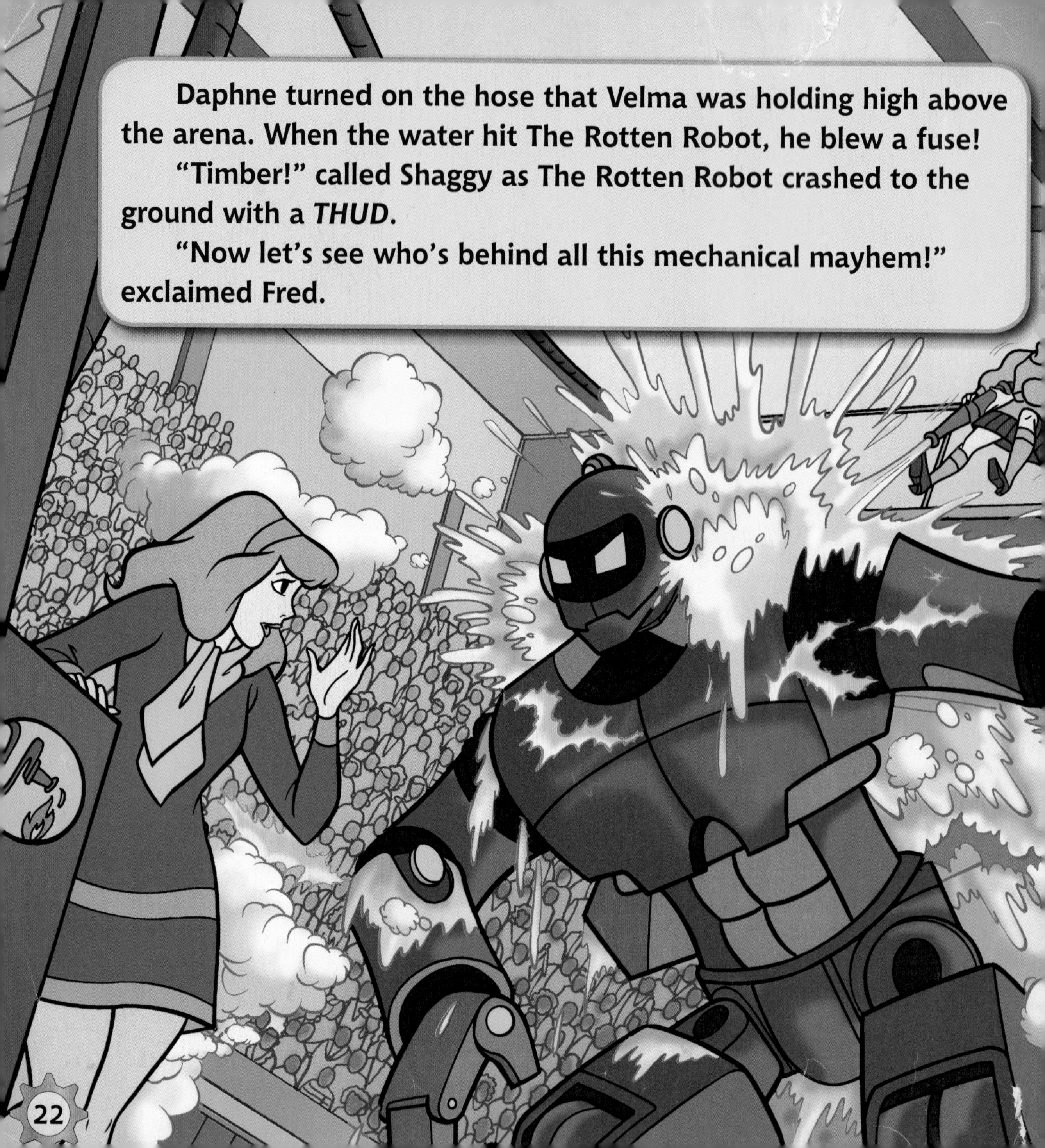
Daphne turned on the hose that Velma was holding high above the arena. When the water hit The Rotten Robot, he blew a fuse!
“Timber!” called Shaggy as The Rotten Robot crashed to the ground with a *THUD*.
“Now let’s see who’s behind all this mechanical mayhem!” exclaimed Fred.

It was Viktor Rustoly! “He reworked the giant Monsterbot so that he could control it from the inside and destroy Doc’s reputation,” explained Velma.

“I could have gotten away with it if it weren’t for you meddling kids and your mutt!” snarled Viktor Rustoly.

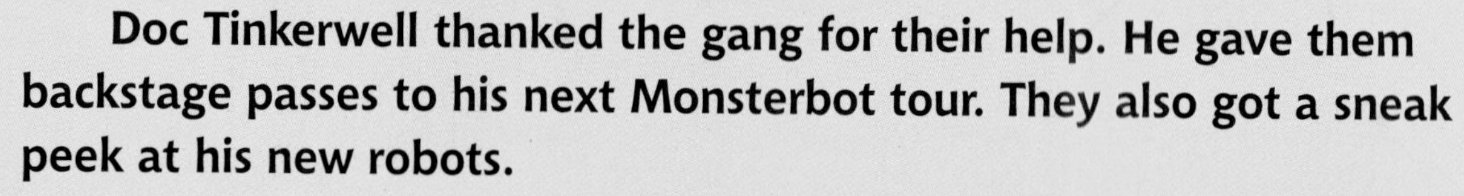

Doc Tinkerwell thanked the gang for their help. He gave them backstage passes to his next Monsterbot tour. They also got a sneak peek at his new robots.

"Like, is it just me, or is there something familiar about those robots?" Shaggy asked. The gang all laughed.

"Scooby-Dooby-Doo!" exclaimed Scooby.